A People in Focus Book

WI1
CHU

Colli

Maxwell Macmill
New York   O>

Acknowledgments

A special thanks goes to The Lady Soames, youngest daughter of Winston Churchill, for making available many of the photographs that appear in this book. The photographs are reproduced through the courtesy of the Mary Soames Collection, Trustees of the Imperial War Museum, Culver Pictures, and UPI/Bettmann Archives. Cover: courtesy of the Winston Churchill Memorial and Library, Westminster College, painting by Allen F. Rader.

Library of Congress Cataloging-in-Publication Data

Driemen, J. E. (John Evans), 1909-
  An unbreakable spirit : a biography of Winston Churchill / by John Driemen.
    p.   cm. (A People in focus book)
  Includes bibliographical references.
  Summary: Examines the childhood, education, war years, political career, and personal life of the British statesman, soldier, and historian.
    ISBN 0-87518-434-0 (lib. bdg.): $12.95
    1. Churchill, Winston, Sir, 1874-1964—Juvenile literature. 2. Prime ministers—Great Britain—Biography—Juvenile literature. 3. Great Britain—Politics and government—20th century—Juvenile literature. [1. Churchill, Winston, Sir. 1874-1965. 2. Prime ministers.] I. Title. II. Series.
DA566.9.C5D75   1990
941.082'092—dc20
[B]
[92]   89-26029
                                                                       CIP
                                                                        AC

© 1990 by Dillon Press, Inc. All rights reserved

Macmillan Publishing Company, 866 Third Avenue
New York, NY 10022

Printed in the United States of America
  2 3 4 5 6 7 8 9 10

Contents

Chapter One	*The Early Years*	5
Chapter Two	*Growing Up*	15
Chapter Three	*Adventures around the World*	23
Chapter Four	*From Pretoria to Parliament*	35
Chapter Five	*Politics and Romance*	45
Chapter Six	*A "Cruel and Horrible" War*	59
Chapter Seven	*In and Out of Government*	73
Chapter Eight	*The Wilderness Years*	83
Chapter Nine	*We Shall Never Surrender*	92
Chapter Ten	*Sir Winston Churchill*	110
Appendix	*Major Events in the Life of Winston Churchill*	121
Selected Bibliography		125
Index		127

Chapter One

The Early Years

The short, stocky man, his shoulders hunched, faced the audience defiantly. He looked like an angry bulldog, ready to attack anyone who threatened his property. His voice rolled across the ancient hall like the roar of waves breaking on a rocky shore. Even a slight lisp could not soften the thunder of his words.

"I have nothing to offer," he growled, "but blood, toil, tears and sweat. You ask," he went on, "'What is our policy?' I will say it is to wage war, by sea, land and air with all our might and with all the strength God can give us...against a monstrous tyranny. You ask, 'What is our aim?' I can answer in one word: Victory—victory at all costs, victory in spite of all terror, victory however long and

Winston Churchill inspired the British people during World War II by the power of his words and his leadership. Here, he makes his famous V for victory sign.

hard the road might be; for without victory there is no survival."

The speaker was Winston Churchill, addressing the British Parliament. At the age of sixty-five, in the midst of a losing war, this old soldier, journalist, author, and politician was taking over the leadership of his country as prime minister.

The date was May 14, 1940. England and France had been at war with Germany since September 1939. They had declared war when Germany invaded Poland. Now Poland had fallen to the Nazi *blitzkrieg* (lightning war). After a long winter lull in the fighting, the French were in full retreat, falling back against the onslaught of the Germans.

Again and again, in speeches to Parliament, on radio carried overseas to the United States, Canada, and the world, the power of his words challenged the enemy. They rallied his battered nation, and stiffened British determination to fight back.

It seemed, in those terrible days, that the only thing that saved Great Britain was the voice and spirit of this determined old warrior. By his words, his leadership, he would guide them—eventually in partnership with the United States and the Soviet Union—to victory. Both the power of his words and his leadership skills would win him a place as one of the great figures of the twentieth century;

perhaps as one of the greatest in human history.

Winston Leonard Spencer Churchill was born on November 30, 1874. It might seem strange that a person would not reach the most important position in his life until the age of sixty-five. In Winston's case, it might seem even more unusual. His ancestry suggested he was destined for greatness.

He was a direct descendant of Sir John Churchill, a general who led the British to a great military victory at Blenheim, Germany, in 1704. A national hero, Sir John was honored as the first Duke of Marlborough. A huge palace, named for his military victory, was built on an estate given to him as a reward for his service to his nation. It was in Blenheim Palace, where his parents were attending a party, that Winston was born. Because he arrived earlier than expected, his birth took place in a coat room. And since no baby clothes were available, he had to be wrapped in towels.

His father, Lord Randolph Churchill, was already a prominent and famous figure. He served as a member of Parliament. One of the youngest men ever to hold a top position in the British government, Lord Randolph was noted for his political speeches. Jennie Jerome, Winston's mother, was an American, and part Cherokee Indian. Considered one of the most beautiful women of her day, she

enjoyed a high social position. The parents of the future prime minister had met in New York City and had fallen in love after a whirlwind romance. They were married in Paris, France, early in 1874.

As with most upper-class English families, Winston saw little of his parents. They were too busy with their own lives. He would later write that he worshiped his mother—"from a distance." He was brought up by a nanny, a full-time nursemaid who cared for him as a baby and throughout his childhood. "It was to her," Winston wrote, "that I poured out my many troubles [as a child] and in my school days." Her name was Mrs. Everest, but he called her "Woom," short for "Woomany." Winston remained as devoted to her as she was to him. Their love for each other continued as long as she lived, well into his manhood.

Three of his early years were spent in Ireland. Lord Randolph had gone there as secretary to his father, Winston's grandfather. The elder Churchill, the ninth Duke of Marlborough, had been appointed by the queen as viceroy, or governor, of that country.

Most of the Irish people resented the English control of their land. Organized groups of rebels, called Fenians, carried on a guerrilla war against the British. From time to time they would bomb

Lord Randolph Churchill, Winston's father.

government buildings and kill British soldiers. Winston never actually saw any of this violence, but it did affect his attitude toward the Irish.

Once, however, when he was out riding a pet donkey, accompanied by his nanny, they were approached by what they thought was a gang of Irish men. They panicked, scaring the donkey. The animal bucked, and the young boy was thrown to the ground. He suffered a bad brain injury. Fortunately, the accident left no permanent damage.

When Winston was five, the family moved back to England. His education began with a governess who gave him private lessons in reading and arithmetic. He loved reading, but he hated doing math problems. What he enjoyed most was playing with his army of toy soldiers. By the age of seven, he had collected almost a thousand of them. Made of lead, about two or three inches high, the soldiers were painted in the bright colors of their real-life uniforms. They were exact miniatures of the army units of the British Empire. Fascinated with military strategy, young Winston used his toy soldiers to create make-believe battles. He played happily, either alone or sometimes with a cousin.

At the age of seven, it was time to enter school. The idea of leaving home terrified Winston. Like most young children of the English

In this photograph, taken when he was five years old, Winston wears a "sailor-boy" suit.

upper class, he went to a "public school." This was really a private boarding school where, except for long holidays, the students lived, attended class, ate, and played—all under strict supervision. Boys and girls did not attend the same schools.

Saint James, the school the Churchills chose for their son, was especially strict. The headmaster had a reputation for using harsh physical punishment. On the dark November afternoon when his mother left him with the headmaster, Winston did not make a good first impression. The man thrust a Latin grammar into the boy's hands. Pointing to to an exercise in the book, he said, "Learn this. I will come back in a half-hour to see what you've learned."

Young Winston had not yet studied Latin, but he had no trouble memorizing and reciting the exercise. Still, he could make no sense of it. Winston demanded to know what it meant. "It says that *mensa* means table," responded the headmaster. "But it also says that *mensa* means 'O, table,' "Why, 'O, table?'" asked Winston.

"That's what you would say," the headmaster answered gruffly, "if you were speaking to a table."

"But I never speak to a table," the youth protested.

The headmaster grabbed the boy and shook him. "If you are impertinent [a smart aleck]," he shouted, "you will be punished severely!"

It was a serious threat. Boys at Saint James were beaten severely for the smallest mistakes, whether in their studies or in their behavior. They would be whipped with tree branches until they bled. Boys who broke the rules were usually punished by beatings in front of the whole student body.

Winston was whipped more than once. His quick mind and independent nature caused many misunderstandings. He especially hated his Latin and Greek classes. "If I had been introduced to these ancients through their history and customs," he wrote, "instead of their grammar, I might have had a better record." His teachers showed little patience with him, and his grades were the worst in his class. Winston's health suffered badly at Saint James. Long spells of stomach upsets and fevers made it even harder for him to keep up with his schoolwork.

After more than two years of misery—and thanks to the begging of his nanny and the advice of the family doctor—his parents finally transferred him to a smaller school near the resort city of Brighton. It was run by two elderly women and was much less strict. Now Winston was able to study French, history, and poetry. He especially loved to memorize and recite poetry. And instead of having to play rough sports such as rugby, he could swim and ride horses, both of which delighted him. He quickly regained his health.

The principals of the Brighton school were also enthusiastic about theater. The school staged many plays. Young Winston played the leading character in a number of these plays. One of his favorites was Robin Hood. He was disappointed that his parents never came to see him act, but his love for drama and theater never faded. Among his favorite gifts as a child was a toy theater from two American aunts, his mother's sisters. During holidays at home, he spent many hours with his model theater. He wrote plays for which he acted and spoke many of the parts himself. Along with his toy soldiers, this gave him another hobby.

Now, too, Winston began to follow his father's career. He cut out stories about his father from the newspapers and collected them. He saved copies of Lord Randolph's speeches and memorized them. And with his remarkable memory, Winston would remember almost everything he memorized for the rest of his life. Although he did not see his father very often, he was very proud of him.

Winston's three years at the Brighton school were happy ones. Then it was time to go on to a school that prepared students to attend a university. His father applied for him to Harrow. Like Eton, Harrow was one of England's most well known private boarding schools. Its entrance requirements were strict and hard. To be accepted, Winston would have to pass several difficult entrance exams. The thought of the exams terrified him—taking them seemed like starting school for the first time.

Chapter Two

Growing Up

Before he could attend Harrow, Winston had to pass exams in Latin and mathematics as well as in other less important subjects. He failed Latin completely. In fact, he handed in a totally blank paper. "I would have liked," he said, "to be asked to say what I knew. They always tried to ask what I did not know."

If he had not been the son of the famous Lord Randolph Churchill, he probably would have been rejected. Because of his family, and despite his failure in Latin, the headmaster made an exception in his case and admitted him into the school.

The twelve-year-old boy paid a price for his poor showing. Students were ranked according to their entrance grades. Winston was placed at the very bottom of the lowest form, or class. At school functions, attended by parents and other guests, the boys marched into the assembly hall according to rank. Winston was the last to enter the hall. Because his family was known to most of the visitors, he could not help hearing their comments about his low standing. He felt a deep sense of shame.

In one way, Winston benefited from his low rank at Harrow. Along with other "slower" students, he was assigned to fewer classes in Latin and more studies in English. According to Churchill, the English master, Mr. Somerwell, "...taught grammar and literature as no one else ever taught it." From this inspiring teacher, Winston acquired a love for, and a command of the English language.

His years at Harrow began badly in other ways than his studies. The school had an excellent swimming pool. Winston had been at Harrow for just a few weeks when, during a play period, he noticed a boy smaller than himself standing near the edge of the pool. As a practical joke, he sneaked up behind the boy and pushed him in.

As it happened, this small boy was a senior, captain of his house, and also the school gymnastic champion. Fully clothed, Julian Amery splashed his way furiously out of the pool, quickly caught

In 1886, twelve-year-old Winston and his mother (front, center) attend a garden party near London.

Winston, and gave him a good ducking. As a result of this prank, Winston acquired a bad reputation with the student body.

But Winston made an opportunity to apologize. He explained that he mistook Amery for a classmate, because he was so small. Then he quickly added, "My father, who is a great man, is also small." Amery laughed and complimented him on his spunk. They became good friends and, in a way, Amery became his protector at the school.

Winston's spunk also caused trouble for him when Mr. Welldon, the headmaster at Harrow, called him in to discipline him for his behavior. "Churchill, I have reason to be displeased with you..." Before Welldon could go on, the boy snapped back, "And I, sir, have a very grave reason to be displeased with you." Again, only Winston's family name probably saved him from more severe punishment.

Young Churchill did get his name into the school records for one outstanding achievement. For an annual contest, he memorized and recited 1,200 lines of *Lays of Ancient Rome*, a poem by the English poet and historian, Thomas Macaulay. On the night before the contest, Winston had memorized 1,000 lines. He learned that he was still 200 lines short of the total needed to win the contest and to set a record. He memorized those overnight. His one disappointment was that his parents were not present to hear and see him win.

    Winston spent four and one-half years at Harrow. During his second year, he had to choose the career he intended to follow, in order to arrange his program of studies. In those days English boys of the upper class had a choice mainly of three professions: the law (and politics), the church (as a clergyman), or the army (as an officer). A career in business, engineering, medicine, or some similar profession was not considered proper for a young aristocrat.

    Winston's choice came about in a curious way. One day at home during a school holiday, he had lined up all of his 1,800 toy soldiers in parade formation for inspection. His father, who was home on a rare visit, agreed to come in and inspect the troops. On the spur of the moment, Lord Randolph asked his son if a career in the army would appeal to him. Winston immediately said yes, and the decision was made.

    For more than three years at Harrow, then, Winston attended the Army Class. Students in this class had to take exams to qualify for Sandhurst, the West Point of Great Britain. A key exam called for the student to draw a detailed map of one of the many British colonies around the world. But which one would it be? Winston wrote the name of the twenty major colonies on slips of paper, put them in a hat, and drew one out. His choice was New Zealand. He memorized everything possible about that faraway land in the South Pacific Ocean. As luck would have it, his exam called for New Zealand. "I hit the jackpot," he said.

At home after graduation from Harrow, Winston had another serious accident. At the time, the family was living on the estate of an aunt, near the English Channel. The house was surrounded by a wild pine forest. Jack, Winston's twelve-year-old brother, and a fourteen-year-old cousin suggested that they play a game of hunters and hunted. The younger boys would be the hunters. Winston would be their prey. They would try to track him down and capture him.

Given a head start, he evaded them for half an hour. Then, winded and out of breath, he found himself trapped on a bridge crossing a deep ravine. His pursuers had both ends covered. Rather than let himself be caught, Winston quickly decided to jump off the bridge. By catching on to the tall trees growing up from the ditch, he planned to lower himself to the bottom and escape.

He jumped, but the tree branches broke under him. Winston fell about thirty feet and landed on hard ground. He was unconscious for three days and in bed for three months with a ruptured kidney. Finally, he recovered and was able to enter the Sandhurst military academy in the town of Aldershot.

Nearly twelve of his eighteen years had been spent in boarding schools. They were not especially happy years. Remembering his boyhood, Churchill later wrote: "I would far rather have been apprenticed as a bricklayer's mate, or run errands as a messenger boy, or helped my father dress windows in a grocer's shop. It would have been real; it would have been natural; it would have taught me more; and I should have done it better. And I would have got to know my father, which would have been a joy to me."

At Sandhurst Winston's attitude toward school changed. Discipline was strict, and the hours of study long and hard. But he had grown up. Courses in military tactics, law, and in mapmaking sparked a keen interest. He also enjoyed drill instruction and classes in horse-riding skills.

Even this was not enough to satisfy his energy. On his own, Winston began to read world and military history, and stories of the great wars of past centuries. He absorbed accounts of military strategy like a sponge absorbs water. The records of the campaigns of Napoleon, a hundred years before his time, held a special fascination for him.

Just before Christmas, 1894, two weeks after his twentieth birthday, Winston Churchill graduated with honors from the military academy. He ranked eighth in a class of 150. Churchill was commissioned a subaltern, a second lieutenant in the queen's army.

But the joy Winston felt at graduation quickly faded. During his two years at Sandhurst, while on leave, he had finally made several trips with his father. Winston had begun to learn about his father's political work, and was eager to contribute in some way.

But even then his father was suffering from a fatal illness. On January 24, 1895, barely a month after Winston's graduation, Lord Randolph died at the age of forty-seven. The death of his father weighed heavily on the young man. He was sure that he, too, would die young. Faced with this sense of doom, Winston felt he would have to crowd many plans and dreams into a very short lifetime. That was his greatest concern as he began his own life, as head of his family, and his own man.

Chapter Three

Adventures around the World

In March 1895, Winston Churchill was assigned to a cavalry unit in the army, the Fourth Hussars. He had joined the regiment earlier, but now, on active duty, his training in horsemanship began in earnest. New young officers trained with their troops and learned to perform many tricks. Riding bareback, they jumped off and on a running horse and guided the horse over a high fence with hands tied behind their backs. The officers also led a company of troops on horseback in and out of complicated formations.

Spills were common. The young lieutenant suffered many bumps and bruises. But though his body may have ached, his enthusiasm never wavered. Winston had a romantic vision of war and

As a young man, Winston Churchill served in a cavalry unit in the British Army.

battle, especially as they had been fought in earlier centuries by professional armies. They were, he thought, "cruel but magnificent," ruled by a special code of honor. Because no war threatened at the time, the young officer worried that he might not see any action.

In the meantime, other, more personal concerns commanded his attention. His beloved nanny, Mrs. Everest, died that same summer. Winston arranged for her funeral and attended to it personally. Though he did not earn much money as a soldier, he left an order for fresh flowers to be put on her grave regularly. Winston kept doing this throughout his life.

The problem of money haunted him. Despite their aristocratic rank, the Churchills had never been wealthy. Lord Randolph had invested in South African gold mines, which in time might have made his family rich. But when he died, the shares had to be sold to pay his debts. Nothing was left. As an army officer, Winston had to pay for his own uniforms and for feeding his horses. He also faced another problem. In those days a British officer was on active duty for seven months of the year, and on leave the other five months. During the five months, he had to support himself.

A rebellion in Cuba at that time caught young

Churchill's attention. Cuba was then ruled by Spain. The Cuban people, weary of Spanish cruelty, had begun a revolution to try to win their freedom. To put down the uprising, more than 80,000 Spanish soldiers had been added to the troops stationed in Cuba. Since he was officially off duty, and since he was eager to experience military action, Winston wanted to cross the Atlantic Ocean and see the war firsthand.

His superior officers gave their permission. Still, it took a lot of pleading and scheming to get the Spanish government to approve the trip. The efforts of an English ambassador, as well as the Churchill family name, helped clear the way. There were strict conditions. The young adventurer would have to pay his own way. Although he would be allowed to carry a pistol and his cavalry sword, combat was forbidden. He could use his weapons only in self defense.

Lady Churchill, his mother, borrowed enough money to pay for his trip. Winston made a deal with the *Daily Graphic*, a leading London newspaper, to write articles from the "battlefront" describing the rebellion. This was the beginning of his career as both a war correspondent and a writer.

With a young fellow officer, Reginald Barnes,

Churchill traveled to New York City in the fall of 1895. They arrived in Havana, Cuba, late in November, but just missed connections with the army detachment that would take them to the scene of some action. Churchill and Barnes proposed going on alone to meet the Spanish general in command. They were told by a friendly officer that their plan was impossible. He was able to work out a route for them with another company of soldiers. Three days of traveling brought them to the main column in the jungle.

Neither of the English lieutenants actually saw the Cuban rebels fight, but they came under fire several times. The Cubans fought from well-hidden positions in the jungle. When attacked, the Spanish troops fired back wildly at unseen targets. Actually, the first time Winston came under fire was early in the morning of his twenty-first birthday. He was sitting alongside a horse when the horse toppled over, shot in the head not a foot away from where Winston was sitting. The experience may have inspired one of Churchill's famous sayings: "In battle, nothing is as exhilarating [exciting] as being shot at without results."

It was his first experience with guerrilla war, and it made a deep impression on him. Although this rebellion failed to win, Churchill predicted that the Spanish could not win either. In 1898, the United States defeated Spain in Cuba to help that country win its independence.

When he returned from Cuba, Churchill rejoined his regiment in India. At that time, India was a British colony, a country completely under British rule. Many army units were stationed there to keep order and to protect government offices and British business enterprises.

Military duty in India was neither hard nor dangerous then. The army day began at six in the morning with an hour and a half of drill. This was followed by a bath and breakfast. From nine to noon, stable duty and paperwork filled the time. Lunch took another hour and a half. Then, everyone slept until five in the afternoon. Almost every evening was spent playing polo or in other recreation. It was an easy life—almost too easy, Churchill felt, although he loved playing polo.

Officers had to pay for their own food, housing, and other needs. Their salaries amounted to $105 a month, plus an extra $15 for the care of their horses. Young officers often shared rented living quarters. Most of them had to get help from their families in England to pay for their living expenses. They would turn over each month's pay to their servants: a boy who took care of their uni-

In India, young Churchill inspects polo ponies, attended by Indian grooms.

forms; a groom for their polo ponies; and a butler who kept house, bought food, and prepared their meals. It was a carefree life.

For young Churchill, this was not enough to satisfy his ambition. He quickly decided he would not be happy spending his whole life as a soldier. In India his education began in earnest, an education he fashioned for himself. He had his mother send him books from England. Without neglecting his military duties or his polo playing—he was the star of his team—he found hours each day to read and study. "A university of one," he called it.

Churchill read the early Greek philosophers: Socrates, Plato, and Aristotle. Among his favorite history books was *The Decline and Fall of the Roman Empire*, by Edward Gibbon. Winston read many books about science, especially the works of Charles Darwin. He also read the books of economists such as Adam Smith and Thomas Malthus. His appetite for knowledge was enormous.

Most of his fellow officers made fun of his study habits. They teased him for being a bookworm. At Harrow, his cockiness had made him an outsider to most of his classmates. In the army, his braininess also made him an outsider. When he tried to share his thoughts—usually in the form of a speech—the other officers often chased him out of the room so they could get on with their card playing or other amusements. Being an outsider never bothered him. Winston knew what he wanted to do with his life; he believed in himself.

Still, he never lost his enthusiasm for military action. Occasional uprisings did occur in parts of India, especially among tribes in remote parts of the country. In the summer of 1897, the Pathan tribesmen in northwest India mounted an armed revolt. The British counterforce was commanded by Sir Bindon Blood, a longtime friend of the

Churchill family. He had promised Winston that he could take part in a campaign if the opportunity arose. Now Winston asked Sir Bindon to keep his promise.

The commander of the Fourth Hussars refused to grant the eager lieutenant a transfer. Finally, he agreed to let Churchill go, not as an active soldier but as a war correspondent. In that role, Winston joined the counterattacking army.

The poorly armed tribesmen had no chance against the superior British forces. While the British quickly defeated the rebels, Churchill made careful notes of each battle. Out of this experience came his first book, *The Story of the Malakand Field Force*, a brilliant and exciting account of Sir Bindon's victory.

The book caught the attention of high-ranking officials in England. Back home on leave, Churchill was thrilled to get an invitation to meet Lord Salisbury, the British prime minister. Lord Salisbury had read and liked the book. He spent almost an hour with the soldier-author, complimenting him on how well the book described life and war in the faraway colony. He offered, in any way he could, to help Winston advance his career.

In the summer of 1898, Churchill asked the prime minister to keep his promise. At this time, colonies in Africa were also part of the worldwide British empire. In the Sudan, south of Egypt, another British army was engaged in putting down a rebellion by the Whirling Dervishes, so called because of their wild, swinging tactics in battle.

These English armies were commanded by Lord Earl Kitchener, who knew and did not like the outspoken Winston Churchill. He refused to accept the lieutenant on his staff. But Churchill's highly placed connections again got him what he wanted. He could join Kitchener's force, but at his own expense, and at his own risk. This time he would be allowed to take part in the action.

At the Battle of Omdurman, Winston rode in the last major cavalry charge of modern times. The horse troops attacked directly into the swarming Dervishes, fighting in hand-to-hand combat. From his horse, Churchill struck down several Dervishes with his sword. He shot another at a distance of less than three feet just as the soldier was about to thrust a spear into his chest. It was a breathtaking experience. Churchill came out of it without a scratch.

His second book, *The River War*, resulted from this firsthand taste of battle. It caused an even greater sensation than the first book. Trying to take advantage of his growing reputation as both a writer and a daring adventurer, Churchill decided to begin the career he had chosen for his life's work—politics. He offered his services as a future candidate for office to the Conservative party, his father's party. Accepting his application, the party leaders assigned him to make a speech in the town of Bath. He would speak to a Conservative club organized there years before by his father.

Winston practiced his speech for hours, especially to overcome a bad lisp. He was able to turn both the lisp and a stutter into effective tools of his speaking style. In his speech, Churchill praised Conservative party principles. He spoke against the ideas of the new, young Labour party and the Liberals who, he said, were always "liberal with other people's money."

His speech won high praise. A columnist for the *Daily Mail* wrote about him: "In years he is a boy; in temperament he is also a boy; but in intention [ambition], in deliberate plan...he is already a man." The same critic predicted that he would be "a great, popular leader, a great journalist, or the founder of a great advertising business."

Winston's speech was a first step toward a career in British politics. While the British system of government is a democracy, it is not quite the same as the American system. Instead of a congress, it has a parliament, also with two groups of legislators. The British House of Commons compares to the United States House of Representatives. The House of Lords is like the United States Senate in some ways, but it has much less power than the American Senate. Members of the House of Lords inherit their seats or are appointed by the king or queen. Members of the House of Commons are elected by popular vote in individual districts. Instead of a president, the British government has a prime minister, who is elected like every other member of Parliament. The prime minister is the person chosen by his or her own party as its leader, and takes office only when that party wins a majority of seats in the House of Commons.

In Great Britain, seats for Parliament often open up in various districts between general elections. These are filled in what are called by-elections. In the summer of 1899, two seats needed to be filled in Oldham, a northern, industrial city. It was a district usually won by the Liberal party. The Conservatives chose Churchill as one candidate, and he ran a spirited and vigorous campaign. Despite his personal popularity, he lost the election.

Winston was not discouraged by the loss. He had experienced and enjoyed his first political campaign. There would be many more to come.

Chapter Four

From Pretoria to Parliament

Full of energy and ambition, Winston Churchill was not the kind of person to waste time worrying about one failure. He constantly looked to the future for new challenges, and his growing reputation as a writer gave him the means to pursue them. His newspaper stories from the battlefronts were producing a steady income. His two books had been best-sellers; they had earned him about $50,000. In those days, that was a small fortune.

Freed from worries about money, Winston could now concentrate on other interests. In 1899, he resigned his army commission and looked for new challenges. A new war in South Africa soon captured his attention. South African president Paul Kruger had challenged the British, who shared much of the region with the Boers, the Dutch Afrikaaners. As a popular writer, Churchill quickly got a job as a war correspondent for the London *Daily Mail*. On October 11, 1899, he sailed for South Africa and into a great adventure.

The conflict between the British and the Boers had a long history. The Afrikaaners were mainly Dutch-speaking people from the Netherlands. They had come to South Africa in the early 1600s, at almost the same time that the Pilgrims from England came to what is now the United States. The Afrikaaners had left their home in Europe to seek religious freedom and to build a new life. Mostly, they became a nation of farmers.

The British came much later, starting a colony in Cape Town at the southern tip of the continent. Led by Sir Cecil Rhodes, the British discovered and developed the rich gold and diamond mines that are still a major part of South Africa's economy.

The two groups of settlers did not get along with each other. In 1881, the Boers took control of the government, but the British kept their industries and many of their army outposts. In the 1890s, the British began complaining about being heavily taxed with no voice in the government. Their battle cry, like that of the American revolutionaries more than a century earlier, was "No taxation without representation." In 1899, open warfare began. Early in the conflict, the Boers succeeded in trapping British garrisons in the cities of Mafeking and Ladysmith.

This was the situation when Churchill's ship landed at Cape Town at the end of October. The fighting was centered mainly at Ladysmith, 700 miles to the north. It took several days by boat and train for Churchill to travel north to the British-held city of Durban.

On November 14, an armored train set out from Durban to Ladysmith under the command of Captain John Haldane. The captain invited the well-known correspondent to come along. Three freight cars with guns and supplies ran ahead of the engine, and several cars with troops trailed behind it. The purpose of this arrangement was to protect the men.

About fourteen miles up the track, the train ran into an ambush. The three cars ahead of the engine derailed, and the whole train came under heavy fire. The frightened engineer tried to run away, but Winston persuaded him to stay. Acting without authority, Churchill took charge. He attempted to get the tracks cleared so that the troops in the rest of the train could escape from the Boers.

In South Africa, Winston Churchill (front, right) was captured and held as a prisoner in a prison camp in Pretoria.

Somehow Winston became separated from the rest of the soldiers. To avoid getting shot, he tried to hide in a ditch. Caught in open country, he was overtaken by a Boer horseman and forced to surrender. Captain Haldane and the rest of the company had also been captured. All the prisoners were marched and transported to Pretoria, the Boer capital, 300 miles to the north. There they joined many other British prisoners of war.

Sixty officers and their batmen (soldier servants) were housed in a school fenced with barbed wire. About 2,000 soldiers were held at a nearby racetrack. Churchill, a natural leader, devised a plan to overpower the Boer guards, free the 2,000 British troops, and seize control of the lightly guarded city of Pretoria. The senior officers in the prison camp vetoed this idea.

Eager to get out, Churchill argued with the Boer officials that he was a war correspondent, not a soldier, and should be freed. British newspapers at Natal, however, had by now printed stories about Churchill's part in the battle of the armored train. The Boers had copies of these papers and refused to let him go. Winston spent his twenty-fifth birthday as a prisoner. But with Captain Haldane and two others, he planned an escape.

After carefully studying the routine of the guards, the British prisoners went into action. At midnight on December 11, Churchill, leading the way, climbed over the fence. He waited for the others. Hearing angry voices, he hid in the shadows. The others could not get out. He could not get back. Stranded in Pretoria, 200 miles from the friendly city of Port Delagoa, a Portuguese colony on the Indian Ocean, he had no choice but to go on alone.

Winston walked in the darkness until he came to a railroad. He hoped to catch a ride on a freight train, but he did not know which direction to take. He would have to trust to luck. After hours of walking, he managed to jump onto a running train, the second one that had passed him. Late the following night, the train stopped, and he got off. In the distance, he saw what he thought were campfires. He decided that these must be fires from a friendly native village. As he came closer, though, the fires turned out to be furnaces working the engines of a coal mine. Two more hours of walking brought him to a cluster of buildings connected to the mine. He was not sure what to do. Making himself known could risk recapture.

Taking a chance, Winston knocked at a door. Finally, a voice cried out in German: "*Was ist da?*" Feeling desperate and trapped, he tried again. The door opened. This time the voice, from the darkness, spoke in English. "What do you want?" Winston offered a wild story about getting lost. When the man behind the door refused to accept the story, the weary traveler identified himself. The man, John Howard, grabbed his hand. "Thank God you have come here. It is the only house for miles where you wouldn't have been handed over. We have heard about your escape; we're all British here, and we will see you through."

Howard, a citizen of South Africa, was an Englishman who was needed by the Boers to run the coal mine. His crew members, all English and Scottish, were also free for the same reason. Churchill had stumbled into the only English settlement in that part of the country.

It was incredibly lucky that he did. Search parties criss-crossed the countryside looking for him. One party of Boer horsemen even came to the coal mine, but John Howard managed to turn them away. For three days and nights, Churchill remained hidden in the mine, in a pit 200 feet underground. Howard and the other members of the crew visited him from time to time to bring him food and encouragement. Most of the time he was alone with packs of white rats.

As the search came to an end, Winston was able to come out of the mine. He continued to hide in a storeroom behind Howard's office until a plan could be worked out for him to escape to safe territory. Late in December, Howard arranged to put him on a freight train transporting wool to Laurenço Marques, the capital of the Portuguese colony. A small, hidden space was fixed for Winston among the bales of wool. He was given a revolver, two cooked chickens, bread, melons, and a jug of cold tea. Three days later, Churchill arrived at the border. He had some scary moments when customs officials took hours to examine the cargo and clear the train. Finally, he felt confident enough to come out of hiding.

Free and safe again, Winston walked down the streets of Laurenço Marques singing at the top of his voice. He found his way to the British consulate buildings. At first, the officials refused to let him in. In his dirty and torn clothing, he probably looked like a tramp. But when he identified himself as Winston Churchill, the staff at the consulate gave him a royal welcome.

The story of his escape caused a sensation in England. Churchill was hailed as a conquering hero. He stayed on in South Africa for several months, covering the war and the lifting of the Boer siege of Mafeking and Ladysmith. His stories and dispatches from Africa were read eagerly, by Americans as well as British readers. They were published in a best-selling book, *London to Ladysmith*.

Arriving back in England in July 1900, Winston was welcomed as a national hero. Only then did he learn that there had been a reward offered for his capture, and that he was once reported to have been caught. If he had been recaptured by the Boers, he would have been shot.

To take advantage of wartime patriotism and

This photograph of Churchill, taken after his escape, shows him beside the overturned train where he had been captured by the Boers.

Churchill's popularity, the Conservative party again asked him to run for Parliament. Winston ran in the city of Oldham, where he had previously lost. The Liberals campaigned hard against him. Liberal newspapers and his opponents tried to portray his escape from Pretoria as an act of cowardice, of deserting his comrades. Their strategy did not work. On October 1, 1900, Winston Churchill was elected as a member of Parliament. His political career had truly begun.

Chapter Five

Politics and Romance

It would be four and a half months before the new member would take his seat in Parliament. Although his income had increased rapidly, Winston now had a chance to earn even more money to support himself in office. In those days, members of Parliament received almost no pay. To serve their country, they had to have other sources of income.

As the hero of the Boer War, Churchill was in great demand as a speaker. In October and November, he toured most of England, speaking four and five times a week to large audiences. He was hailed and honored, much like an athlete who has won a great victory. For each speech, he was paid from $500 to $1,500. Winston was able to save much of what he earned. With this money, he would be able to devote most of his attention to his new duties.

An American promoter, Major Pond, arranged an American and Canadian tour for him. In December 1900, Churchill crossed the Atlantic Ocean for the second time, to speak to American audiences about his wartime experiences. His international reputation was growing swiftly. Major Pond introduced him as "the hero of five wars, the author of six books, and the future prime minister."

Churchill himself was more impressed by the man who introduced his lecture in New York City—the famous American author, Mark Twain, who wrote *Tom Sawyer* and *Huckleberry Finn*. "Having an English father and an American mother," Mark Twain said, "makes Mr. Churchill a perfect man." Twain also gave the young Englishman a complete set of his books. He signed them with this saying: "To be good is noble; to teach others to be good is nobler, and no trouble." It was a motto Churchill would never forget.

In New York, he renewed his friendship with a leading American politician, Bourke Cockran. The two had met when Winston passed through New York on his way to Cuba five years earlier. An Irishman educated in France, Cockran had moved

Winston Churchill in 1900 during his speaking tour of the United States and Canada.

to the United States as a young man. He had become a successful lawyer and a prominent figure in both city and national politics. He was considered one of the greatest orators, or public speakers, of his day.

Cockran had a strong influence on Winston, whom he treated almost as a son. He shared many secrets of oratory with the younger man. Cockran took Churchill with him to watch a murder case in court, where he pointed out: "To present a case [in law or politics] you have to pick the strongest argument and concentrate on that…"

The American leader also influenced Winston in another way. Politically, Cockran was a liberal. He believed in free trade between nations and that government had a responsibility to help poor people. He thought the way the British treated the South African Boers was wrong. Most of these ideas were opposed by Churchill's Conservative party. Swayed by this powerful and eloquent American, Winston began to have second thoughts about his own political views.

During Churchill's tour of the United States, not every audience was enthusiastic. Irish Americans especially, who had sided with the Boers and resented British control of their homeland, greeted him angrily. By making jokes at his own expense and showing sympathy for the Boers, he was able to calm their anger. Mostly, his American tour was a great success.

On January 22, 1901, England's Queen Victoria died after reigning for sixty-four years, longer than any monarch in world history. The new king, Edward VII, called for Parliament to begin its new session in mid-February. On the second of that month, the day the queen was buried, Churchill sailed for England from Boston. On February 14, he took his seat in Parliament for the first time.

New members were expected to wait two or three months after being sworn in before making their first speech. Winston was too impatient to wait that long. He had prepared his speech in the United States and practiced it on the voyage back home. In Parliament, he faced a challenge. He was used to speaking by reading from a written paper while standing behind a podium. This was considered bad form in the House of Commons. So he not only wrote his speech; he memorized it. It was also his habit to collect and keep notes of witty remarks to be used whenever they fit. He had a collection of these in readiness. His first speech would be about his experiences in South Africa, with a plea that the government make a generous peace with the Boers.

Only three days after taking his seat, Churchill asked to be recognized by the Speaker of the House. Instead, the Speaker gave the floor to David Lloyd George, leader of the opposing Liberal party. Lloyd George was expected to offer an amendment, a change in a law that was being debated. Instead, to the surprise of everyone, Lloyd George gave a speech attacking government policy in South Africa and the tactics of the British military in the war. This was the very theme that Winston had chosen for his speech.

When Lloyd George finished, the Speaker recognized Churchill. There was no escape; he would have to speak. As he hesitated, another member sitting beside him whispered a suggestion: "Make a joke about Lloyd George's change of topic." Acting on the suggestion, Winston began, "If the honorable member [Lloyd George] instead of making his speech without moving his amendment had moved his amendment without making his speech... ." Applause and laughter greeted the new member. His wit had won the house to his side. He, too, spoke about the Boers, asking for kindness for them so they could continue their way of life. Although many members of his own party disagreed with his ideas about South Africa, his speech won high praises from most of the press, and from leaders of both political parties. Churchill's disagreement with his party about South Africa was just the beginning of many differences. Germany, in those days, was building a huge army and navy and challenging other European nations for world power. In response, the Conservative secretary of war, William Broderick, had begun a campaign to strengthen the British army. Churchill was equally concerned with the growing German threat. But he felt that as an island nation and a worldwide colonial empire, Great Britain should concentrate most of its resources on its navy. To match Germany, he thought, would be to turn England into a military nation. That, he feared, might break down the country's democratic traditions.

On the home front, he became the ringleader of a small group of rebels who opposed other Conservative party policies. The opinions of his American mentor, Bourke Cockran, were also beginning to affect Churchill's thinking. As a liberal, Cockran was a champion of working men and women. Although by birth and upbringing, Churchill belonged to England's upper class, he, too, began to feel a growing concern for the working and housing conditions of many English workers. Once, he lashed out at his own party leader. "Mr.

Chamberlain," he said, "loves the working man; he loves to see him work."

Remembering his nanny, Mrs. Everest, and her loneliness and poverty in old age, Winston campaigned for and helped establish pensions. Such programs meant that old people would have comfort and security when they could no longer work. His short stay in the prison camp in Pretoria led to an interest in English prisons, where conditions as he saw them were bad. Churchill was able to get laws passed to improve the prisons. He never hesitated to voice his opinions and to act in support of them.

But the big break with his own party came in March 1904. Churchill criticized the government's budget as wasteful, especially because it called for spending more on the army. In the middle of a speech he was making on this point, the prime minister and other members of the cabinet walked out of the House of Commons to show their disapproval. A month later, in his last speech as a Conservative, he spoke in support of the rights of workers to organize unions. Conservative newspapers called him a "radical."

Winston refused to back down on policies he believed were right for the nation. On May 31, 1904, he entered the House of Commons. Instead of taking his usual seat, he crossed the aisle to sit down with the Liberals, next to David Lloyd George. The following year, the Liberals won the election and took control of the government. The new prime minister, Mr. Campbell Bannerman, rewarded Churchill with a seat in the cabinet: undersecretary of state for the colonies. In that election, Churchill barely held his seat in Parliament from Manchester, a longtime Conservative city.

When, following the general election, the new prime minister died suddenly, his place was taken by Henry Asquith. A shift of positions took place in the cabinet. Lloyd George moved up to become chancellor of the exchequer, Asquith's old job. Churchill was promoted to Lloyd George's office as president of the board of trade, a position like that of secretary of commerce in the U.S. government today.

Now, because he had officially changed parties, British law required Churchill to run again in a special election. At that time, the suffragettes—women campaigning for the right to vote and run for office—were gaining political strength. They were very active, marching in the streets, and chaining themselves to the gates of Parliament. These women broke up many political meetings by shouting down candidates whom they opposed.

Churchill and other Liberal party members were targets for such protests because the party did not support giving women the right to vote. Although Winston personally supported the suffragettes, and although they could not vote against him, their demonstrations helped defeat him in Manchester. British election law, however, allowed him to run again almost immediately in a by-election in a different district. This time, he ran in the strong Liberal city of Dundee, Scotland, and won handily.

While campaigning in Dundee, Winston met Clementine Hozier. She was in the audience when he gave his keynote speech. They had met earlier that year, very briefly, at a social affair. Now, at a dinner party after the rally, they had an opportunity to get to know each other.

Clementine came from a politically active, strongly liberal family. She was born into an upper class, Scottish family, but like some others in her class, she was poor. To support herself, she had to work as a governess, tutoring and caring for the children of the wealthy. She was impressed with the fiery young orator and with his ideas about the responsibility of government to help the poor rise out of poverty.

Winston was thirty-three, and Clementine, twenty-three, tall, beautiful, and stately. The young

Clementine Hozier and Winston Churchill at the time of their engagement.

politician was strongly attracted to her. She had a keen mind—a mind finely tuned to political subjects. She and Winston were in agreement on many issues. They discovered they had much in common, and not only in politics.

Winston fell completely in love with Clementine. Fascinated by his conversation, by his dynamic personality, and the promise of greatness that she felt in him, she came to love him, too. Some months after their meeting in Dundee, at a party in Blenheim Palace, they were caught out in the garden during a summer storm. They found shelter in a gazebo, and there Winston proposed to her. On September 12, 1908, they were married in Westminster Abbey, the most famous church in London. During all the exciting, challenging, and often difficult years of his life, Clementine was the one who stood by her husband, and gave him the strength to go on. Of her he said, "I married and lived happily ever after."

It was a happy marriage. In the years before World War I, Winston and Clementine had two children: Diana, in 1910, and Randolph, born two years later. Sarah was born just after the start of the war in 1914. Four years later, Clementine gave birth to another daughter, Marigold. In 1922, Mary, the last of the Churchill children, was born.

In 1913, Clementine accompanies Winston, now first lord of the admiralty, for the launching of the H.M.S. Iron Duke, a British warship.

From 1908 to the outbreak of war, Winston Churchill served in a variety of high-ranking government posts. He continued to fight for working-class people. He was active in getting laws passed to raise minimum wages and to reduce working hours. But in 1910, as home secretary in the cabinet, Churchill called out the army to break a strike by Welsh coal miners. Labour party members bitterly opposed this action.

It was a time of change in Europe. Germany was building up its military power. German forces threatened England and France in North Africa, and at the Suez Canal in Egypt, then under British control. In 1911, Germany sent a battleship to Morocco in a show of strength. France and England joined together in protest, and this time Germany backed down. A growing number of British government officials argued that more money should be spent on the military and less on public welfare for the poor.

Churchill was caught in the middle. But as a soldier who clearly saw the coming of World War I, he, too, supported an increase in military strength. In his various cabinet positions, his energy and drive had led him into activities that normally belonged to other departments. Other cabinet secretaries resented and complained about his meddling. But in 1913, Henry Asquith, the prime minister, appointed Churchill first lord of the admiralty—the secretary of the navy. Winston was now in a position to exercise real power.

Chapter Six

A "Cruel and Horrible" War

For several years, conflicts among nations had brought Europe closer to war. Germany, which in the 1800s had been made up of several small kingdoms, had become a united country ruled by an emperor, Kaiser Wilhelm II. Like England and France, Germany owned colonies in Africa and Asia. Now, with growing military might, Germany wanted to become a leading world power.

In the hidden struggle for top rank, nations began to form alliances against each other. On one side, Germany allied itself with the Austrian-Hungarian Empire, which included some of the Balkan states and Turkey. On the other side, loosely joined together, were Great Britain, France, Russia, and Italy.

As first lord of the admiralty, Churchill worked closely with admiral of the fleet Lord Fisher to prepare the British Navy for World War I.

No one in the British cabinet was more keenly aware of the threat of war than Winston Churchill. He plunged into his job as first lord of the admiralty with the energy and enthusiasm of an athlete preparing for a championship game. Traveling aboard the navy yacht, *Enchantress*, he visited every ship in the fleet.

To modernize the ships of the world's greatest navy, Churchill changed their power plants from coal burning to oil. Using oil for fuel would enable them to be refueled at sea instead of coming ashore. That way they could stay in action longer. Churchill increased the size of the guns on the big battleships from thirteen to fifteen inches, to give them more range and firepower. He ordered the fleet to practice war games to make sure they would be ready for whatever happened. And he did everything possible to improve the living and working conditions aboard ship.

Foreseeing, in 1912, the part that airplanes would play in future wars, Churchill added an air branch to the navy. He called for an air force to "defend Britain's harbors and oil tanks."

In 1913, at the age of thirty-eight, Winston took flying lessons and became a skilled pilot. Shortly before he would have won his wings, his instructor died tragically in a crash. In those early days of aviation, planes were not as reliable as they are today. They crashed frequently. Flying was extremely risky and dangerous. Clementine, now expecting their third child, begged Winston to give up flying. He agreed, although he would continue to co-pilot many flights in later years.

All his preparations proved to be wise strategy. On June 28, 1914, in Sarajevo, Serbia (now Yugoslavia), a seventeen-year-old Serbian youth shot and killed Archduke Ferdinand Charles of Austria and his wife Katharine. It was the spark that set off

In April 1914, Churchill boards a seaplane in the harbor at Portsmouth, England.

the explosion of World War I. Austria declared war on Serbia. Russia was an ally of Serbia. France had a treaty to come to the aid of Russia, and Germany, France's bitter enemy and Austria's ally, declared war on both Russia and France. England had pledged to fight to defend its allies.

Long before this, Churchill had outlined the general strategy for the war. He was convinced that Germany's first move would be to invade and try to crush France. Without waiting for his government to declare war, he ordered the British fleet into battle stations. When Germany invaded neutral Belgium as a way to get to France, England did declare war. Because the navy was ready and in position, there would be no surprise attack on England. The British government and the people congratulated Churchill for his daring.

Three years earlier, Churchill had written an article predicting the early course of the war. "[France]," he wrote, "will not be strong enough to invade Germany. Her only chance to conquer Germany will be in France." He went on to predict that twenty days after the invasion, the German armies would defeat the main French armies at the Meuse River, in eastern France.

The march would then continue to the Marne River, about forty miles from Paris. There, Churchill predicted, the German armies would be so stretched out that the French would be able to stop them. This would happen, he said, on the fortieth day of the offensive. Three years later, that is exactly what happened. On the forty-first day of the actual war, Germany lost the Battle of the Marne. Then the war on the western front in France settled into a bitter stalemate. When Churchill's paper first appeared, army staff members called it "ridiculous and fantastic." Now they had to admit they were wrong.

But Churchill's war record suffered some defeats as well. The first of these occurred at the city of Antwerp in Belgium early in the war. Invaded by the Germans, Belgium called for British help. Churchill himself led a small company of English marines to Antwerp to stop the German march to the French port of Dunkirk. He arrived, dressed in a fancy admiral's uniform, riding in a limousine and leading a parade of London double-decker buses carrying the British troops. It looked more like a holiday celebration than a military action. Since he found the Belgian army in complete disorder, Churchill took command.

This token attempt to stop the German armies failed. Churchill and his troops barely escaped. The English newspapers called the affair the "Antwerp Circus," and Churchill's enemies criticized him harshly. Defending himself, Churchill declared that to win wars, risks had to be taken. He was aware of the consequences of failure, but refused to run away from them or make excuses. Still, for a long time, Antwerp would be remembered as a tragic defeat for the British and for Churchill.

Later, he would have to shoulder the blame for an even worse military tragedy. Turkey had entered the war on the side of Germany by attacking Greece. Also, the Turks controlled the Dardanelles, a narrow strait near the city of Constantinople (now Istanbul). Because the Dardanelles was the gateway to the Black Sea and Russia, the Allies could not ship needed military supplies to the Russians. To remove this blockade and gain control of the strait, the Allies would have to attack Turkey.

Lord Kitchener, now commander-in-chief of all the British armed forces, suggested a naval attack on the Dardanelles. Churchill strongly supported the idea. Military experts agreed that defeating the Turks and strengthening Russia on the second front in the east would greatly shorten the war.

There was a hitch. Churchill worked out a plan for a naval bombardment combined with a landing and invasion by seaborne troops. Kitchener convinced the cabinet that a surprise attack by ships alone would be enough. Against his own judgment, Churchill sent a fleet of battleships to attack the Turks. A fierce bombardment lasting weeks failed to break through Turkish defenses. The element of surprise was now lost. Germany had time to send reinforcements to help its partner.

Eventually, Kitchener did send troops—mostly

Australians—to the scene. They landed on the beaches of a peninsula called Gallipoli. High above the beaches, the well-armed Turkish armies could look down at the Allied troops and pin them down under a murderous assault of firepower. For nine months, through most of 1915, the British and Australian forces tried in vain to storm the ramparts above Gallipoli. Several thousand Allied soldiers were killed or wounded. Finally, they gave up.

Churchill accepted the blame for the disaster. To prevent a collapse of the ruling Liberal party, Liberal leaders had to invite the Conservatives to join them in a national government. As their price for this compromise, the Conservatives demanded that Churchill be dismissed from the cabinet. In November 1915, he resigned in disgrace. It was a low point in his life.

Clementine refused to let her husband feel sorry for himself for long. Though she herself was deeply troubled, she kept up a show of good cheer that helped restore Winston's self-confidence. While he continued to serve as a member of Parliament, he discovered a new activity to lift his spirits—oil painting. Winston was encouraged to start by his sister-in-law, Lady Gwendeline Churchill. Clementine was quick to buy him the paints, brushes, and canvases he needed to pursue what became his "passionate hobby."

Playing with his children—Diana and Randolph and two of his nephews—also became one of Winston's pleasures at this time. Their favorite game was Bear, a kind of hide-and-seek. While the children closed their eyes, their father would climb and hide in a tree. Then, when they came looking for him, shouting, "Bear! Bear!" he would jump out of the tree without warning and chase them until he caught them. Father and children never tired of this game.

But the war continued, and Churchill was a professional soldier and a patriot. In November 1915, at his own request, he went back on active duty as a major with the Grenadier Guards. At the time, this unit was stationed at the front battle lines in France, in an area of heavy fighting.

The war had turned into an endless battle that neither side could win. The countryside was in ruins from the constant shelling. Both the Allied soldiers and the Germans were dug in, in long lines of trenches, sometimes within shouting distance of each other. Barbed wire guarded the outer rim of the trenches. Troops ate, slept, lived, and died in these pits. Front line officers lived in caves dug into the trenches. These dugouts were covered

with sandbags to give them protection from incoming shells.
 For the soldiers, life in the trenches was sheer misery. In winter they slept in mud, water-soaked, surrounded by swarms of rats. From time to time, one side would bombard opposing troops with long-range shellfire, and then sent the infantry "over the top" to attack on foot. Millions of soldiers on both sides died without either side gaining an advantage.
 Churchill shared the misery with the troops under his command. Several times he narrowly escaped death. Once, a message from his commanding general caused him to leave the front lines for a meeting. When he returned two days later, his dugout was a shambles, completely destroyed by German shellfire, and two of his officers had been killed. It was then that he changed his opinion about war. Instead of "cruel and magnificent," he described it as "cruel and horrible."
 The front-line battles would continue for months and years. As relief from the misery and the killing, Churchill turned again to his hobby of oil painting. Actually, he did his painting right in the battle zones. During lulls in the fighting, he would paint scenes of destruction—shell holes, for example—caused by an artillery barrage. For Win-

ston, it was a way of keeping up his spirits.

During Churchill's months at the battlefront, he and Clementine exchanged letters almost every day. Their letters—delivered promptly because of his importance—were filled with their love for each other. She would write, for example, "My Darling, I miss you terribly. I ache to see you. When do you think you might get a little leave? Shall I come and spend it with you in Paris?" His letters told the same story. "My Dearest One," he wrote, "I have your little photograph [near my heart] and kiss it each night before I go to bed." In addition to exchanging messages of love, Clementine also kept Winston well informed about what was going on in the political world.

After six months, Churchill resigned his commission to return to London. He made the decision in part because his command ended when his battalion was combined with another unit. Also, Lloyd George and other leaders felt he would be more useful in government. Churchill had, while at the front, written some reports criticizing British military strategy. Among other ideas, he proposed developing an armored vehicle that later became known as the tank. He believed it would save the lives of many foot soldiers.

Technically, Churchill did not "invent" the

During World War I, Churchill speaks to a group of munitions workers.

tank. But it was his idea to build a military vehicle that could travel on caterpillar tracks. Moving in this way, it could cross over ditches and any kind of land, go through barbed wire, and act as a moving fortress for the infantry. In England, the idea was called "Churchill's Folly." But when the first ones were built, sent into action, and drove the German troops back in panic, the tank ceased to be a "folly." The new weapon became a powerful instrument of war.

In April 1917, the United States, which had

remained neutral, entered the war on the side of the Allies. This greatly increased the Allied chances for victory. Now, too, because the war had been going badly, David Lloyd George replaced Henry Asquith as prime minister. Despite the objections of the Conservatives, the Liberal leader brought Churchill back into the cabinet as minister of munitions. In this new assignment, he would work closely with Bernard Baruch, a well-known American in a similar position. They would become close friends.

In his new job, Churchill had to travel back and forth frequently by plane between England and France. On one occasion, crossing the English Channel, the engine of the plane failed. The pilot turned back toward France. Just before they were about to crash into the sea, the engine sputtered to life. Winston and the pilot managed to land back in France. They tried again in a second plane. It, too, experienced engine failure, but they did glide to a landing on the English coast. As Churchill wrote: "I was a bit late for my London engagement."

His excellent work with the American forces was rewarded by a medal—the Distinguished Service Cross—presented to him by General John Pershing, the American chief of staff. Churchill was the only Englishman so honored.

American power turned the tide. German troops launched their final drive in March 1918, using poison gas for the first time. Despite terrible casualties, the Allies, led by the Americans, stopped their advance. Soon, the German armies fell back in a disorderly retreat. On November 11, 1918, the war finally ended. And although few people noticed at the time, seeds of dramatic change had been planted in the world. Winston Churchill would play a major part in the shape of those changes.

Chapter Seven

In and Out of Government

Churchill's job did not get any easier with the end of World War I. The tireless leader directed the operation that brought millions of soldiers home from the battlefront and returned them to civilian life. He also took charge of some Allied troops that stayed in Germany, Turkey, and the Middle East to help rebuild the ruins of war.

Although Churchill was only one member in a government of many people, it seemed at times that he alone was responsible for solving the major problems. Critics accused him of trying to be too important. That did not stop him. He tackled his duties with great zeal and energy.

A problem that commanded much of his attention was the "Irish question." Then as now,

Ireland was split. A Catholic majority in most of the country favored independence. But a Protestant majority in the five northern counties known as Ulster wanted to continue as part of Great Britain. To avoid civil disorder in England's "back yard," Churchill had helped work out an agreement promising home rule to Ireland after the war. Despite a rebellion in 1916 by Irish Catholics and continued unrest, this agreement kept Ireland under control during the big war in Europe.

In 1920, the time had come to act on this promise. Now, as secretary of state for colonies, Churchill took on the role of peacemaker. The Irish leader with whom he negotiated was Michael Collins, a fierce fighter for the Catholic cause. The two men started out as enemies. They ended up as warm friends.

Churchill and Collins agreed to make Ireland a dominion, a partly independent country like Canada and Australia. Not all the Irish people were happy with the treaty. As he himself had predicted, Collins was assassinated by his own people. But before his death, he wrote: "Tell Winston that we could never have done this without him." Through their negotiations, Irish independence—except for the five counties of Ulster—finally became a reality in 1923. But the trouble in Ulster between the

Protestant majority and the Catholic minority continues to this day.

Churchill also played a key role in the postwar shaping of the Middle East. For centuries, Turkey had controlled this region, cradle of three great religions: Judaism, Christianity, and Islam. During these centuries, the Islamic people, mostly Arabs, had been ruled by the Turks. In return for supporting the Allies, Great Britain had promised to help the Arab nations, including Egypt, gain independence from Turkey.

A soldier and friend of Churchill, T. E. Lawrence, organized an Arab revolt in Egypt and led them to victory. He became famous as "Lawrence of Arabia." England kept its word to the Arabs, but this was complicated by another promise. In 1917, the British government had issued the Balfour Declaration. This was a promise to build a Jewish homeland in Palestine, the land of the Bible.

No one was a stronger supporter of this idea than Churchill. He believed that the Jews, who had lived in exile for almost 2,000 years, should be helped to return to their religious homeland. He also thought that a Jewish state in this strategic area would give Great Britain a vital military advantage.

In 1921, Churchill and officials from other governments created the states of Iraq and Trans-Jordan out of the old Turkish empire. He arranged to put two members of the royal Arab family, the Feisals, on the thrones of these new countries. Churchill hoped that their moderation, loyalty, and gratitude would help to satisfy the ambitions of the Arabs. He also hoped that this arrangement would make it possible to establish a Jewish state in Palestine without creating a conflict between Arabs and Jews.

These achievements were overshadowed by two personal tragedies during that same year. In June, his mother suffered a bad fall and died. In August, his youngest daughter, Marigold, only three years old, died suddenly. Clementine and Winston were shocked and deeply saddened. Clementine hid her grief in order to support her husband, who showed his feelings more openly. For several weeks, they canceled all their public activities and retreated to Scotland. There, as he did in times of stress and sorrow, Winston turned to his easel to paint. Painting helped him work out his grief.

In 1922, unsettled conditions in Great Britain made it necessary for the Liberals to call a new election. Churchill ran again as a Liberal in Dundee, but an attack of appendicitis kept him from campaigning. The Liberals lost the election, and

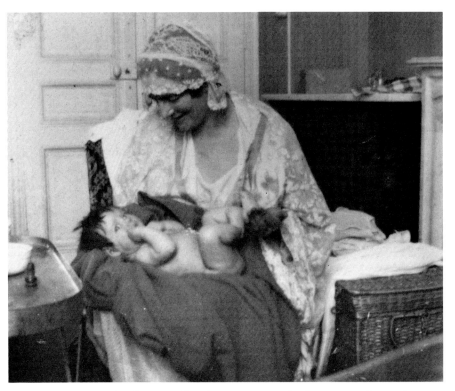

After the death of Marigold, Clementine gave birth to Mary, her and Winston's fifth and last child. Here, Clementine holds Mary after giving her a bath.

Churchill also lost. For the first time in twenty-two years, he was out of office.

Being out of Parliament gave him time for other activities. More than most upper-class Englishmen, Winston enjoyed being with his children. He delighted in organizing games and various activities for the children and his nephews and nieces, playing with them as though he himself were a child.

Winston had time, too, to look for a permanent home for his family. Over the years, the

Churchills had moved several times. Clementine accepted every move with cheerful patience. A small inheritance now made it possible for Winston to buy a home of their own. He fell in love with an estate in Kent, called Chartwell. In November 1922, Winston drove his family to the estate. Like a child springing a surprise, he announced that this was their new home. Clementine did not like the house, but she kept her disappointment to herself. Though she had just given birth to their last child, Mary, she worked with her husband to turn Chartwell into a true home.

The manor house, actually a small castle, was run-down. Still, it commanded a magnificent view of lawns and woods. With Clementine's help, Winston began to restore the house and put the grounds in the best of shape. In the process, he built many decorative walls, and would sometimes lay bricks just for the fun of it. He became so good that the bricklayer's union made him a member.

Now, too, Winston started several major writing projects. The biggest one at the time was a six-volume history of World War I, *The World Crisis*. Instead of writing by hand as he had done early in life, he now dictated to a secretary. Hour after hour, puffing his big Cuban cigars, he would pace the floor, speaking about the events of the war.

Afternoon naps gave him the energy to work until two or three in the morning. In time, he would use several secretaries in shifts. Only after they had typed out his dictation did the author sit down at a desk to revise and to add new ideas.

Two years of this busy life did not lessen Churchill's desire to get back into active politics. In 1923, as a Liberal, he lost another election at West Leicester. Changing his position again the following year, he asked the Conservative party to take him back so that he could run for Parliament in London. When the party turned down his request, he started his own party—the Constitutionalists—and ran as an independent.

Churchill's campaign created a sensation. It broke all the British traditions of reserve and dignity. Instead, it borrowed from the flash and glitter of American politics. In a district that included both upper-class aristocrats and working-class people, Churchill enlisted the help of rich women, stars of the English theater, and athletes. All of them volunteered their time and effort. Winston himself traveled the streets in a horse-drawn carriage, broadcasting his message through a megaphone.

Never had he enjoyed a campaign more. He even enjoyed matching wits with hecklers in the streets. To a socialist who kept interrupting him, he shouted: "If this man tried to interrupt a speech in Russia, he would wind up in jail." Despite the enthusiasm created by his army of celebrities, he lost this election, but only by forty-three votes.

His strong showing and spirit won for him the support of Lord Arthur Balfour. The former prime minister wanted to see Churchill's "brilliant gifts of public discussion" back in Parliament on the Conservative side. He convinced party officials to forgive Churchill and to assign him a seat in the city of Epping where the Conservatives always won. Not only did the "hop-skipping" politician return to Parliament, but the new prime minister offered him a cabinet position: the chancellorship.

At first Churchill thought that Stanley Baldwin meant a mostly honorary position. Actually, Baldwin wanted Churchill to serve as chancellor of the exchequer, the second most powerful position in the cabinet. The job, a prominent writer said, "...had the prestige of a U.S. Chief Justice [of the Supreme Court], with the combined power of the U.S. Secretary of the Treasury...and the Chairman of the Federal Reserve [Bank]." Winston had now achieved the same rank—at the age of fifty—that his father had occupied almost forty years earlier.

As chancellor, Churchill planned government budgets, decided where to spend money, and set the taxes to cover spending. The job did not really fit his talents. Even worse, the 1920s were not the best of times, financially, in England. World War I had weakened Great Britain's economy and the country's industries. Still, Churchill tackled the job with his usual vigor.

Because of the difficult times, he became a favorite target for critics of the government. To the Labour party, which was gaining strength as the times grew worse, Churchill was a "reactionary," an "enemy of the working man." The Liberals labeled him a turncoat, a traitor. In 1926, while he was in office, a general strike swept the country. Much of the labor force—miners, railroad and factory workers, truck drivers, newspaper reporters— quit work. When the strike paralyzed the country, Churchill had to act to end it. As finance minister, he took most of the blame for all that, in the opinion of the opposition, was wrong.

Winston, as usual, openly faced the challenge. In fact, despite his critics, he helped create the British social security system. In 1925, he worked to pass a law that provided government benefits to more than a million poor people. Through all the insults directed at him, he never lost his sense of humor. In one speech to Parliament, he counted up the number of times he had been accused by his opponents of "robbery, betrayal, outrage, infamy, burglary, villainy, and so on."

In 1929, as a worldwide depression began to affect Britain, the Conservatives had to call a general election. When the Labour party won, Ramsay MacDonald became prime minister for the second time. Churchill kept his seat in Parliament, but he was no longer a cabinet minister. In disfavor with his own party, he had become once again a lonely outsider. "If it weren't for the chance that someday I might be prime minister," he said, "I'd quit politics altogether."

Chapter Eight

The Wilderness Years

From 1929 to 1939, troublesome times spread across the world. The Great Depression made life hard for the citizens of Great Britain, the United States, and most other countries. Millions of people were out of work, homeless, and hungry. In Germany, Adolf Hitler and his Nazi party rose to power. In Asia, Japan used its growing military strength to expand its influence and control.

Now in his fifties, Churchill worried about the way the British people—and especially their leader, Ramsay MacDonald—seemed to be losing their spirit. Politically, those ten years were the most trying in his life. The Conservatives joined the winning Labourites in a national, or union government, but both parties turned their backs on him. Churchill could not agree with their common policies. He no longer had any official position. Several writers called this period his "wilderness years."

Although Winston was no longer a leader in the British government, his tremendous drive and energy expressed itself in other ways. After the election, he traveled to Canada and the United States. With him he brought along his son, Randolph, now eighteen, his brother Jack, and Jack's son. The four Churchills had a great time touring Canada, fishing, riding horses, and most of all, enjoying the love of the Canadian people. Canadians hailed their visitors as heroes.

From Canada, Winston visited Hollywood in California. He met and became friends with many movie stars—especially with Charlie Chaplin, the famous comedian. He met William Randolph Hearst, publisher of many newspapers. They did not agree politically, but they did become friends. Churchill wrote many articles for the Hearst newspapers.

While in California, following the advice of a stockbroker, Churchill invested almost all of his money in American stocks. Not long afterward, in New York on the way back to England, he witnessed the great stock market crash of October

Winston in Canada in 1929 with his son Randolph (left), his brother Jack (right), and Jack's son.

1929. From his hotel window, Winston saw a man who had lost his money jump to his death. Churchill, too, lost almost everything in the crash. His wartime American friend, Bernard Baruch, helped Churchill save part of his investments.

Winston now turned to writing to make up for the money he had lost. In 1931, two of his books were published: the final part of his six-volume history of World War I, and also the story of his growing up, *My Early Years*. Like most of his books, they were very popular. He also began work on a four-volume history of the English-speaking people. And he signed a contract to write a biography of his famous ancestor, John

Randolph, the Duke of Marlborough. Along with his many newspaper and magazine articles, his writing enabled him to prosper again.

Winston's work habits were unusual. Typically, he began his day with an enormous breakfast in bed, often including soup, fruit, cheese, roast beef, chicken, kippers (fish), and even champagne. He would dictate letters and take care of political business, also from bed. Then he took a hot bath, and began his writing from the bathtub by dictating to a secretary sitting just outside the bathroom door. Dictation continued until lunch, another big meal. After relaxing in his garden, Winston returned to dictating. Later, he took an afternoon nap and another hot bath. Evenings he spent with Clementine. When she went to bed at eleven, and guests who had shared their huge evening meals were gone, Winston resumed writing. Again, he dictated to secretaries until two or three in the morning. This was a routine he followed regularly, especially when working on a book.

Winston needed all his strength for such a schedule, because he needed all the money he could earn to pay for his expensive life style. Twice a year, he vacationed—sometimes with Clementine, sometimes with friends—in France, mostly to paint. Every painting session featured a picnic

Winston and Clementine in the early 1930s.

lunch that most people would consider a banquet: wine, champagne, and gourmet food.

Winston liked to drink as well as to eat. His political enemies spread rumors that he was a drunkard, an alcoholic. These charges amused Winston. In fact, he bragged about his drinking. Considering the number of important books he wrote, all his other writing, and his tireless political activity, few people took these charges seriously. If the 1930s were "wilderness years" politically, they were, for Churchill, not unhappy years.

Albert Einstein, a famous scientist, visits Winston Churchill in the rose garden at Chartwell during the 1930s.

But there was much more to his life during this time than travel, writing, painting, and the enjoyment of family and friends. The threat of war in Europe and the world greatly concerned him. Churchill felt that British leaders were ignoring the growing danger of the German threat. From his seat in Parliament, in his magazine articles, and from speaking platforms, his voice rang out loud and clear. Continually, he pointed out the weakness of the government, including his own party leaders.

After taking power in Germany, the Nazi leader, Adolf Hitler, began to demand military equality with the rest of Europe. (German arms had been severely restricted by World War I treaties.) The British government responded to Hitler by proposing that all nations cut back their armies and reduce their armaments. At one time, Ramsay MacDonald even offered to set an example for Germany by disarming Britain.

To Churchill this was a foolish and dangerous response to German demands. He was convinced Hitler could not be trusted. Churchill was especially concerned about the buildup of Nazi air power compared to the weakness of the British air force and defense. When German aircraft helped destroy the Spanish republic in that country's civil war in 1937, it only confirmed Churchill's fears. He criticized the prime minister, Stanley Baldwin, for insisting that "there was no defense against an air attack." Baldwin said that the only hope for peace was in disarmament, "which also had the advantage of costing much less."

Churchill was able to challenge the cabinet because, with friends and supporters, he organized what his opponents called a "shadow, or secret government." Lord Beaverbrook, owner and publisher of Britain's largest newspaper, supported

Churchill's stand. A young and upcoming politician, Brendan Bracken, became his assistant. Ralph Wigram, a brilliant officer in the foreign service who kept track of the German air force, turned to Churchill when his superiors ignored his reports. Wigram explained how the Nazis had designed their civilian aircraft to be converted quickly to military use. A neighbor, Major Desmond Morton, gathered information for Churchill about German industry and military preparations. Wing Commander Torr Anderson, an officer in the Royal Air Force (RAF) kept the "shadow prime minister" informed about the terrible condition of British air defenses.

With great care and accuracy, Churchill built his case for a stronger Britain. The events that followed only strengthened Churchill's warnings. In 1937 Germany annexed Austria. Early in 1938, Hitler demanded independence for the Sudeten region of Czechoslovakia. The Sudetens were German people who had lived peacefully in Czechoslovakia since that country became independent after World War I. They had no quarrel with the Czechs.

Although the Sudetens agreed to accept an offer of more political freedom, that did not satisfy Hitler. In September 1938, Neville Chamberlain, the new British prime minister, flew to Munich, Germany, to meet with Hitler and negotiate a deal. Without allowing the Czechs to take part in the meetings, Chamberlain agreed to all of Hitler's demands. Sudetenland became part of Germany. In fact, Hitler had no real interest in the Sudeten people. What he really wanted was the Skoda armament factories in Czechoslovakia, then the biggest in the world. Early in 1939, the Nazis marched in and took over the whole country without firing a shot.

When Chamberlain returned to England after his meeting with Hitler, he waved a sheet of paper at the crowd that greeted him at the airport. It was an agreement he had signed with the Nazi leader. "Peace in our time," he cried out in triumph. Not peace, Churchill warned, but surrender. In Parliament he challenged Chamberlain: "You were given the choice between war and dishonor. You chose dishonor and *you will have war!*"

Chapter Nine

We Shall Never Surrender

When Hitler seized all of Czechoslovakia, the mood in Britain changed. Churchill's warnings were coming true. English newspapers, and much of the public, now clamored for his return to the cabinet. But Chamberlain still refused to listen, even when members of his own party began resigning. A few critics said Chamberlain was afraid that Churchill would push him into the background. The prime minister insisted that Hitler would soon be satisfied. Events quickly proved him wrong.

Now Hitler turned his attention to Poland. He demanded the return of the Polish port of Danzig (now Gdansk), which had been returned to Poland after World War I. In July 1939, Germany and the Soviet Union, once bitter enemies, shocked the

Winston Churchill makes one of his famous radio speeches, broadcast by the British Broadcasting Corporation (BBC).

world by signing a treaty in which they agreed not to fight each other. Churchill predicted that Hitler's demands for Polish land and the treaty with the Soviets signaled a coming German invasion.

On August 8, Churchill broadcast a speech to the United States. He reminded Americans of what happened twenty-five years earlier in 1914: the German invasion of Belgium. Then he warned of the coming of war. In a way, his speech forced Chamberlain to sign a treaty with Poland to defend that country if attacked.

On September 1, Hitler's armies marched into Poland. His air force began a crushing attack on that country. For almost two days, Chamberlain hemmed and hawed, demanding that the Germans stop. They paid no attention to him. On September 3, England and France declared war on Germany and its ally, Italy.

Now there was no way to keep Churchill out of the cabinet. The British people demanded his return for the confidence his strength offered. According to a popular saying of this time: "While Chamberlain wrings his hands [at the Nazi treachery], Churchill shakes his fist." The old warrior was reappointed first lord of the admiralty, in charge of the navy. Throughout the fleet, signal flags flew, and radio messages went out: "Winnie is back! Winnie is back!" The wilderness years were over.

There was little either the British or the French could do to help Poland. The German air force destroyed its cities, and German tanks overran the country. In little more than three weeks, Poland lay crushed. In keeping with the terms of their treaty, Germany and the Soviet Union divided the country between them.

With the fall of Poland and the coming of winter, the conflict turned into what came to be called "the phoney war." Nothing happened. The French forces, joined by British armies, waited behind the 300 miles of concrete forts and guns of the Maginot line in northern France. For months, no major action took place.

On May 10, 1940, the "phoney war" ended. Instead of attacking the Maginot Line, the Nazis struck through the Netherlands and Belgium, just as they had in World War I. German tanks and planes quickly crushed all resistance. Chamberlain had to resign as prime minister. He tried to get his friend and defense minister, Lord Irwin Halifax, to replace him. His own party gave him no choice. Now it had to be Winston Churchill.

"That night," Churchill would later write, "as I went to bed at about 3:00 A.M., I was conscious of a profound sense of relief. At last I had the authority to give directions over the whole scene. I felt as if I were walking with destiny, and that all my past life had been but a preparation for this hour and this trial...I was sure I should not fail. Therefore, although impatient for morning, I slept soundly and had no need for cheering dreams. Facts are better than dreams." At the age of sixty-five, he had reached his life's goal and his greatest challenge.

The new prime minister quickly formed a

cabinet made up of the leaders of all three political parties. Anthony Eden, a Conservative, directed the war office. Sir Archibald Sinclair, the Liberal leader, headed the air ministry. Clement Atlee, the Labour leader, became Churchill's second in command. Churchill added to his own duties the job of minister of defense.

Winston Churchill's first speech to Parliament as prime minister began a series of the most powerful and inspiring messages ever delivered in the English language. "I have nothing to offer but blood, toil, tears and sweat...." he began. And he called for "victory at all costs...for without victory there is no survival."

"To Churchill," wrote James Hume, an American writer, "words were weapons and speeches deeds." The power of his words would be proven dramatically in the days and years to come. In Britain, the speech lifted the spirits of the people and filled them with courage for their desperate battle against the Nazi military might.

On May 16, Churchill flew to France, now reeling under the force of the German attack. When the French generals appealed to him for planes to fight the Nazi air force, he had to refuse. British planes, outnumbered by the Germans at least five to one, would be needed for the defense

In summer 1940, Churchill meets soldiers who are stationed at a coastal defense position near Hartlepool, England.

of the British Isles. But to bolster French morale, he offered British citizenship to all Frenchmen.

On June 2, the British armies were trapped on the beach of Dunkirk, in France, just across the English Channel from England. More than 300,000 troops faced death or capture. Again using the power of words to rally the English people, Churchill directed an almost impossible rescue. The whole nation responded bravely. For twenty-four hours, more than 800 boats—navy vessels, private yachts, sailboats, motor boats, even rowboats—

crossed back and forth across the thirty-mile-wide channel to save the army. Somehow, the air force was able to limit the German attack during this rescue. The army lost all its weapons, but the troops were saved.

After Dunkirk, Churchill spoke again to the English people. "We shall defend our island whatever the cost may be...we shall fight on the beaches, we shall fight on the landing grounds, we shall fight in the field, we shall fight in the hills...we shall never surrender!" And to a colleague sitting beside him he whispered, "And we'll fight them with the butt end of broken bottles because that's bloody well all we've got."

In Washington, President Franklin Roosevelt listened to Churchill on radio. Roosevelt turned to his assistant, Harry Hopkins, and said, "Whatever we give to England will not be money down the drain. As long as that old so-and-so is in charge, England will never surrender."

On June 14, the German armies marched into Paris. France surrendered. A month later, Hitler made a "peace offer" to England—peace on German terms, which meant complete control of British life by the Nazis. Too scornful to reply in person, Churchill had Lord Halifax (now ambassador to the United States) broadcast his refusal.

Now Britain braced for a Nazi invasion. In the face of this danger, Churchill made another famous speech. "The Battle of France is over," he said, "I expect the Battle of Britain to begin. Upon this battle depends the survival of Christian civilization…if we fail, then the whole world, including the United States, including all we have known and cared for will sink into the abyss of a new Dark Ages…[so] let us brace ourselves to our duties, and so bear ourselves that, if the British empire and its Commonwealth last for a thousand years, men will say, 'This was their finest hour.'"

Perhaps because of Churchill's defiance, and despite England's military weakness, the invasion never came. Instead, the Nazis attacked with their air force. By destroying the British air defenses and the outnumbered planes of the Royal Air Force, as well as much of England, Hitler was sure he could force the country—and Churchill—to surrender.

The Battle of Britain began in late August 1940. In September, the Nazis launched a massive air attack on London and other major cities. All twenty-five RAF squadrons rose into the skies to meet the invaders. There were no reserves. Many RAF pilots flew as many as eighteen hours a day. Their valiant effort was rewarded. After British Spitfire planes shot down fifty-six enemy bombers in one day, the German planes turned back. Praising the brave pilots, Churchill made this now famous statement: "Never in the field of human conflict was so much owed by so many to so few."

That was only the beginning. Night and day, German bombers attacked London and other British cities. London turned into a city of ruins. Parents sent their children to the countryside, as far as possible from the city. Those who could not leave spent much of their time underground in the city's subway system. Over the autumn and winter, more than 100,000 British civilians died from the bombings. Huge fires swept across the cities, adding to the death and destruction.

Churchill worked tirelessly to lift the spirits of the English people. During bombing lulls, he went out into the wreckage to comfort them. Their cheers brought tears to his eyes. Seeing him weep, they cheered all the louder. "He cares! He cares about us!" they shouted. In response, he would raise his hand in a signal that has lived on to this day—the V for victory sign.

The victory sign, probably invented by Churchill and certainly first used by him, began in this way. Each night, the British Broadcasting Corporation (BBC) opened its radio newscast with a musical theme: the first bars of Beethoven's Fifth Sym-

After a German bombing raid, Churchill inspects the ruins of Coventry Cathedral.

phony. The first notes are three short and one long. In the Morse wireless code, three dots and a dash stand for the letter V. Churchill combined these symbols into a gesture by raising his hand and forming a V with the two forefingers of his hand. In this way, he saluted the crowds. Ever since, this sign has been used by people campaigning for a cause to show their belief in victory.

By the spring of 1941, the German air raids became less frequent. But England was still in terrible danger. The war effort—the manufacture of

In late September 1940, Winston and Clementine travel down the River Thames by launch to visit areas of London that had been hit by German bombs.

arms and planes—suffered from lack of material and money. Food was in short supply and had to be strictly rationed. Much of what the country depended on came across the Atlantic Ocean from the United States and Canada on the ships of the British Merchant Marine. Many of these ships were sunk by German submarines, the U-Boats.

In desperation, Churchill turned to President Franklin D. Roosevelt of the United States. In answer to Churchill's plea for some idle American destroyers to protect British merchant ships,

Roosevelt arranged a loan of fifty destroyers. Called Lend-Lease, this program gave a big boost to British morale. Because the president believed that Churchill would never allow England to be beaten, he arranged for the military aid while the United States was still officially neutral. Although many Americans opposed getting involved in the war, the prime minister's speeches convinced most of them that the British deserved their support.

Heard in Germany, those speeches may have changed Nazi strategy. In July 1941, the Germans turned away from England and, despite their treaty, invaded the Soviet Union. Churchill had long before predicted this move. In fact, he had tried to warn Stalin, the Communist leader. Now he believed that the Soviets' need to survive would make them a valuable ally, and take some of the pressure off of Britain. He offered his help immediately. When his secretary, knowing how much the prime minister hated communism, asked how he could join forces with Stalin, Churchill answered: "If Hitler invaded Hell, I would make at least a favorable reference to the Devil in the House of Commons."

Events moved swiftly. In August, Churchill crossed the Atlantic in the British battleship, the *Prince of Wales*, to meet with President Roosevelt.

Together, the two leaders worked out an eight-point document they called *The Atlantic Charter*. The charter was a plan for the peace that would follow victory, for the United Nations organization, for world freedom, and for preventing future wars. Churchill and Roosevelt became close friends. They would meet often to plan joint strategies for both war and peace.

On December 7, 1941, Japan attacked and sank most of the American Pacific fleet at Pearl Harbor, Hawaii. The next day, the United States declared war against both Japan and Germany. The attack shocked Churchill no less than his American friends. But his reaction was swift. "We're in the same boat now," he wrote, adding later, "I went to bed [that night] and slept the sleep of the saved and thankful." With the United States now a partner in the war, he was more sure than ever of victory.

Shortly after the attack on Pearl Harbor, Churchill returned to Washington, D.C. He pleaded with Roosevelt to fight as hard in Europe as he knew the president would against Japan. Churchill stayed as a guest in the White House. Once, the president, who had to use a wheelchair because his legs were paralyzed by polio, wheeled into Winston's room just as he came out of a bath. There he was, completely naked, a cigar in one hand and a drink in the other. The embarrassed president turned to leave. "Please stay," his guest said, "His Majesty's First [Prime] Minister has nothing to hide from the President of the United States."

On the same visit, Churchill spoke to the members of Congress. It was one of his greatest speeches. The squat, bulky figure of the English "bulldog," whose words rang out with determination and passion, captured the hearts of everyone who heard him. He received the greatest ovation of his life. Remarkably, with all his duties and responsibilities, he managed to write every word of his own speeches—possibly the only world leader of modern times to do so.

Encouraged by his American reception, Churchill pushed for an ever greater effort in England. The wartime situation began to take on a more hopeful outlook. In the winter of 1942, the Soviets had finally stopped the Germans at Moscow and at Stalingrad (now Volgograd). In North Africa, British General Bernard Montgomery had swept out of El Alamein in Egypt to defeat the Germans, commanded by Field Marshal Erwin Rommel. It was England's first major victory. "Not the end," Churchill said, "not even the beginning of the end. But it is, perhaps, the end of the beginning." The

United States, too, had begun to push back the Japanese in the Pacific. In 1943, Churchill returned to Washington twice to meet with Roosevelt to plan the invasion of Allied troops—the forces fighting against Germany and Italy—in Europe. There were many other trips: to Teheran in Iran to meet with Stalin; to Cairo, Egypt; and to Casablanca in North Africa for another meeting with Roosevelt. Although Churchill risked his life by flying to these meetings, he was tireless in his pursuit of victory. In planning for the Allied landing in Europe, he argued for a sweep through Greece and the Balkan nations. American troops had already landed in Italy and were driving back the German and Italian forces.

Churchill wanted to invade through eastern Europe to prevent the Soviets from gaining control of that region. Although the Soviet Union was an ally, he still distrusted Stalin. But the Americans, led by General George C. Marshall, the chief of staff, and General Dwight D. Eisenhower, supreme commander of the Allied forces in Europe, decided that an attack across the English Channel into France was a better idea. In the end, Marshall and Eisenhower prevailed. They planned to launch the crossing in early June 1944, depending on the weather.

Wearing his famous "siren suit," Winston Churchill meets with General Dwight D. Eisenhower a few weeks before the D-day invasion.

D-Day, as it came to be known, turned out to be June 6. On that morning, with the invasion already under way, and with great secrecy, Churchill addressed Parliament. "I have to announce," he said, "that during the night and early hours of this morning, an armada of 4,000 ships, together with several thousand smaller craft, crossed the [English] Channel..." It was his way of breaking the big news.

Actually, he had planned to cross the English Channel himself with the first landing wave of soldiers. General Eisenhower would not permit it, but it took the king of England to keep the seventy-year-old prime minister at home. If Churchill sailed, the king told him, then the king would also go. Still, six days after D-Day, Churchill did cross the channel and toured the battle zone for seven hours with General Montgomery before returning home.

It would take ten more months for the war in Europe to be won. There would be still more traveling for Churchill: to Quebec City in Canada for another meeting with Roosevelt; to France; to Moscow to meet with Stalin; and again to Yalta in the Soviet Union to plan for the postwar peace with both Roosevelt and Stalin.

On April 12, 1945, President Roosevelt died suddenly from a brain hemorrhage while vacationing in Warm Springs, Georgia. A shocked and deeply saddened Churchill said, "He died on the wings of victory...but he saw the wings and heard them."

On April 30, Hitler, in his underground bunker in Berlin, took poison and shot himself in the mouth. A week later, on May 7, Germany surrendered. The war in Europe was over.

Later, an aide to Churchill figured that the prime minister had traveled "more than 125,000

Winston Churchill (seated, left), Franklin D. Roosevelt (seated, center), and Joseph Stalin discuss their postwar plans at Yalta.

miles on wartime missions, had spent more than 800 hours at sea, and 350 hours in the air." How important was Churchill's contribution to victory? In many ways it was beyond measure. But General Omar Bradley, one of the top American military officers in Europe, put it simply. "Every one of his speeches," General Bradley said, "was equal to an army [of 15,000 men]."

Chapter Ten

Sir Winston Churchill

With the war finished in Europe, much remained to be done. American forces were still fighting against the Japanese in the Pacific. In August 1945, the United States defeated Japan with the help of two atomic bombs that destroyed the cities of Hiroshima and Nagasaki. A system of peace and a plan for rebuilding the ruins of Europe had to be established. For this purpose, Churchill met with Harry Truman, the new American president, and Joseph Stalin. The three world leaders gathered at Potsdam, Germany, in July 1945. Stalin demanded that several eastern European countries—Poland, Hungary, Rumania, Bulgaria, Czechoslovakia, and part of Germany—be put under Soviet control to help protect the Soviet Union against possible future

Winston Churchill, Harry Truman (center), and Joseph Stalin join hands during their conference at Potsdam, Germany.

attacks. Churchill objected, but he soon realized that England alone could not change the plans of the two bigger and more powerful nations.

At Potsdam, he received an even more disturbing piece of news. His Conservative party had lost a new election. Although he kept his seat in Parliament, his party no longer had a majority. The Labourites, led by Clement Atlee, had won. That meant that, nearing the age of seventy-one, he was no longer the prime minister. It was a bitter blow. Clementine, thinking of his age and the terrible strain of the war years, called it a blessing in disguise. Answering her, he said, "At the moment, it seems quite effectively disguised."

How could the great hero who had led his nation and much of the world from disaster to victory be rejected by his own people? Many political experts agreed that it was not really a defeat for Winston Churchill personally, but for his party. He had been critical of the Labour party leaders. He believed that their socialist ideas, such as having the government own and operate major industries, were not good for the country. Churchill had not campaigned very hard against Atlee. Now, with the war won, the English people were more concerned about jobs, pensions, medical care, housing, and other down-to-earth problems.

Whatever the reasons, the results of the election affected him in an unusual way. For several months, he was deeply depressed. The queen wanted to make him a nobleman, but he turned down this offer. To accept a title of this kind, he would have to resign from Parliament, and he was not ready for that.

Early in 1946, an invitation from President Truman to speak at a ceremony at Westminster College in Fulton, Missouri, lifted him out of his depression. In the United States, people everywhere greeted him like a conquering hero, a champion. Wherever the train stopped—from Washington, D.C., to Jefferson City, Missouri—crowds gathered to cheer him.

In his speech at Fulton, the great orator gave the language another memorable phrase. Speaking about the possible threat posed by the Soviet Union and the spread of communism, he compared the situation to the events leading up to World War II. That war, he said, "could have been prevented...without firing a single shot." But no one would listen; no one would act.

"Now," he said in his speech, "a shadow has fallen upon the scenes so lately lighted by the Allied victory...From Stettin in the Baltic [a German city] to Trieste [an Italian city], an *iron curtain* has descended across the continent." Churchill worried about what might happen to the people behind that "iron curtain," now controlled by the Soviet Union. At first, American leaders responded to the speech with disapproval. Only later did its meaning become clear. And like many other phrases invented by Churchill, *iron curtain* would become part of the English language.

With a new cause to promote, anti-communism, the old leader resumed his dynamic, energetic life-style. Now, too, he could enjoy spending time with Clementine and his four grown children. To indulge his passion for painting, he traveled to France, to Italy, and to Africa. He started another major writing project, a six-volume history of World War II and his years as prime minister.

Churchill received many honors. On January 3, 1950, *Time* magazine featured him on the cover (for the seventh time). It named him not just "Man of the Year," but "Man of the Century." Later, Churchill would be honored with the Nobel Prize for literature for the many books he had written. He was as busy as ever. Along with his anticommunism campaign, he had plans for a United States of Europe, and plans for improving living conditions in Great Britain without socialism.

Surprisingly, Churchill's political career had not yet ended. After four years of a Labour government, the English people grew tired of socialism. They voted the Conservatives back into power. As leader of his party, Churchill once more became prime minister. On his seventy-fifth birthday, just before taking office again, a crowd of reporters and photographers gathered outside his London home. One of the photographers spoke up. "I hope, sir, that I will shoot your picture on your hundredth birthday." His wit as sharp as ever, Churchill snapped back, "I don't see why not, young man.

Winston Churchill makes an official visit as prime minister to Queen Elizabeth and her two young children, Prince Charles (right) and Princess Anne.

You look reasonably fit and healthy."

The years of his second term as prime minister were not nearly as eventful as the first. Still, there were some notable accomplishments. Churchill returned important industries, such as steel and mining, from government to private ownership. He led the country to prosperity. When King George V died, Churchill played a prominent role in the coronation of the new monarch, Queen Elizabeth II. In a way, this event framed his political career. Beginning in the reign of Queen Victoria in 1900, he would finish it under a second queen.

Churchill found the strength to recover from a stroke. Soon afterward, he called for a summit meeting—the first time this phrase was used. Churchill proposed a conference between the heads of government of the United States, Great Britain, France, and the Soviet Union to strengthen world peace. President Eisenhower refused to include the Soviets at the meeting on the Atlantic island of Bermuda. But out of this first summit came the idea, and then the formation, of the North Atlantic Treaty Organization (NATO).

Though Winston refused to accept a nobleman's title, he did accept a lesser honor from the new queen: Knight of the Garter. That entitled him to be called Sir Winston Churchill, like the first Sir Winston, the father of the Duke of Marlborough. Still another unusual honor took place during the celebration of his eightieth birthday. Breaking all tradition, the celebration was held in the House of Commons. There, Winston received many gifts. By now, though he had been re-elected as leader of his party, he felt the time had come for him to resign. He had long ago promised to turn over the leadership to Anthony Eden. "I must retire," he announced with his old wit, "Anthony won't live forever."

On April 4, 1955, the night before he would leave Number 10 Downing Street, Queen Elizabeth came to pay tribute to her prime minister. It was the first time in British history that a king or queen had honored a commoner—a person who is not of noble rank—in this way. The queen, it was clear, did not consider Sir Winston a common person.

Churchill was re-elected to Parliament again that year, but he would no longer be very active in politics. Still, he maintained a busy schedule, continuing to paint, to write, and to travel. In 1959, he came to the United States to visit President Eisenhower and to say, in his words, "goodbye to the land of my mother." Two years later, he returned on a private yacht owned by Aristotle Onassis. As the yacht anchored in New York Harbor, President John F. Kennedy phoned Sir Winston to invite him to visit the White House. But word had come that Clementine was ill. Winston declined the president's invitation in order to return at once to England. At the airport for the flight home, a big crowd of American well-wishers gave him a rousing send-off. Two years later, President Kennedy, by an act of Congress, named him an honorary citizen of the United States. It was the first time that such an honor was ever given to a foreigner.

In July 1964, Churchill appeared in Parliament

for the last time, not to make a speech but to say good-bye. He had to be helped to his seat. The current prime minister, Harold MacMillan, paid him a special tribute: "However long he lives, you will never see his like again." Later that summer, Dwight Eisenhower came to London to visit his old comrade, now sick in a hospital. The two wartime leaders did not talk much. They simply held hands in loving friendship. As they said good-bye, Churchill managed to raise his hand to give, once more, the old V sign for victory.

On his ninetieth birthday, November 30, 1964, Sir Winston was able to come to the window of his London home to accept the cheers of the crowd gathered outside. He received good wishes from world leaders and from thousands of ordinary people. One was simply addressed to "the Greatest Man in the world."

On Saturday, January 9, 1965, about six weeks after his birthday, the old warrior refused—for the first time—his nightly drink and cigar. Years before, he had predicted that he would die on January 24, the same date on which his father had died. Like so many of his other amazing predictions, this one also came true. At eight o'clock on Sunday morning, January 24, 1965, seventy years after his father's death, Sir Winston Churchill died.

Sir Winston Churchill.

The writer James Humes described the final tribute as "not so much a funeral as a festival celebrating the greatness of one man's humanity." Funeral services were held in Saint Paul's Cathedral. From there the body was carried by motor launch on the River Thames to Waterloo Station. Then it went by train to the Bladon churchyard near Blenheim Castle, where Winston was buried beside his father, mother, and brother.

Along with the hundreds of thousands who followed the procession, the millions around the world who watched on television, and the flight overhead of the RAF pilots, perhaps the greatest tribute to this great man came from the dock workers lining the riverbanks. As the launch rode by on the river, one after another, the workers dipped the huge boat cranes in salute. It was an unplanned gesture, a message of love that spoke for people everywhere in the free world.

In his memoirs, Churchill offered as his motto the following words:

> In War: Resolution
> In Defeat: Defiance
> In Victory: Magnanimity
> In Peace: Goodwill

In a way, that is how he lived his remarkable life—a life that, with all his human faults, contributed as much to liberty and freedom as any in world history.

Appendix

Major Events in the Life of Winston Churchill

1874	Winston Spencer Churchill is born at Blenheim Palace near London
1884	Churchill begins formal schooling at Harrow
1894-95	Churchill graduates from Royal Military College at Sandhurst in December. Commissioned Second Lieutenant in the Fourth Queen's Own Hussars, April 1895
1895-98	Churchill observes war in Cuba; on army duty in India and Africa
1899	Churchill runs for Parliament for the first time, as Conservative candidate for Oldham; loses election
1899	Churchill serves as war correspondent in South Africa; is captured and imprisoned; escapes prison in Pretoria, South Africa

1900	Churchill is elected to Parliament as Conservative party member from the city of Oldham
1908	Churchill marries Clementine Hozier
1904-15	Churchill holds various positions in the cabinet of the governing Liberal party; First Lord of the Admiralty
1914	World War I breaks out in Europe; Germany attacks France; England declares war, August 4, 1914
1915	British naval attack against Turkey at the straits of the Dardanelles fails; Churchill is blamed; resigns as First Lord of the Admiralty
1915-17	Churchill serves in front lines of the war in France as colonel in the Grenadier Guards
1917	Churchill rejoins cabinet of new prime minister, Lloyd George, as minister of munitions
1918	World War I ends; Armistice is signed on November 11
1919-22	Churchill serves in various cabinet positions; as colonial secretary, leads negotiations in Ireland and Middle East

1922	Churchill loses election; is out of Parliament for the first time since 1900
1924	Churchill switches back to Conservative party; is named Chancellor of the Exchequer in the cabinet of Prime Minister Stanley Baldwin
1930-39	Churchill continues as member of Parliament, but disagreement with his party on military and other policies make him an outsider; he warns about the dangers of the rise of Naziism in Germany and the threat of a new war in Europe
1939	World War II begins, Germany invades Poland; on September 3, England and France declare war on Germany; Churchill is called to join cabinet of Prime Minister Neville Chamberlain, again as First Lord of the Admiralty
1940	Germany invades Norway, the Netherlands, and Belgium. Churchill becomes prime minister; he rallies country to defy Germany as German air force batters England in the Battle of Britain
1941	Churchill crosses the Atlantic Ocean to meet with U.S. President Franklin Roosevelt to sign Atlantic Charter

1941	Japan attacks Pearl Harbor, Hawaii, on December 7; the United States declares war on Japan and Germany
1942-45	Churchill travels extensively to lead Britain to victory in war; meets with Roosevelt and Joseph Stalin
1944	June 6 is D-Day; Allies invade Europe
1945	President Roosevelt dies on April 12; on May 7, Germany surrenders; Conservative party loses in general election; Churchill resigns as prime minister; on August 14, Japan surrenders; World War II ends
1951	Churchill becomes prime minister for the second time; he resigns in April 1955
1963	Churchill is named an honorary citizen of the United States by President John F. Kennedy
1965	Churchill dies in London on January 24, the seventieth anniversary of the death of his father, Lord Randolph Churchill

Selected Bibliography

Adler, Bill. *The Churchill Wit.* New York: Coward McCann, 1965.

Brendon, Piers. *Winston Churchill, A Biography.* New York: Harper & Row, 1984.

Butterworth, T. *The World Crisis.* New York: Charles Scribner's Sons, 1951, 1959.

Callahan, Raymond A. *Churchill: Retreat from Empire.* New York: Scholarly Resources, 1984.

Churchill, Winston S. *Amid These Storms.* New York: Charles Scribner's Sons, 1932.

———. *My Early Life.* New York: Charles Scribner's Sons, 1958.

———. *Great Destiny.* New York: G. Putnam's Sons, 1965.

———. *A History of the English Speaking People.* New York: Dodd Mead, 1965.

———. *Memoirs of the Second World War.* Boston: Houghton Mifflin, 1959.

Colville, John. *Winston Churchill & His Inner Circle.* Boston: Wyndham Books, 1981.

Eade, Charles. *The End of the Beginning: War Speeches by Winston Churchill*. Toronto: Cassell, 1943.

Gilbert, Martin. *Churchill*. New York: Doubleday & Company, 1980.

———. *Winston Churchill: The Wilderness Years*. Boston: Houghton Mifflin, 1982.

Halle, Kay. *Irrepressible Churchill: A Treasury of Winston Churchill's Wit*. New York: World Publishing, 1966.

Humes, James Co. *Churchill: Speaker of the Century*. New York: Stein & Day, 1980.

Kimball, Warren F. *Churchill & Roosevelt: Correspondence*. Princeton: Princeton University Press, 1984.

Manchester, William R. *Winston Churchill: The Last Lion*. Boston: Little, Brown, 1988.

Soames, Mary. *Family Album: A Personal Selection from Four Generations of Churchills*. Boston: Houghton Mifflin, 1982.

Taylor, J.P. *Churchill: Four Faces & The Man*. New York: Dial, 1973.

Woods, Frederick R. *Young Winston's Wars: Original Dispatches*. New York: Viking Press, 1973.

Index

Asquith, Henry, 53, 58, 71
Atlantic Charter, The, 104
Atlee, Clement, 111, 112
Baldwin, Stanley, 80, 89
Balfour, Lord Arthur, 80
Balfour Declaration, 75
Baruch, Bernard, 71, 85
Battle of Britain, 99-100, 101
Battle of Omdurman, 32
Blenheim Castle, 119
Blenheim Palace, 7, 56
blitzkrieg, 6
Blood, Sir Bindon, 30-31
Boer War, 36-37, 45
Chartwell, 78
Chamberlain, Neville, 90-91, 92, 95
Churchill, Clementine Hozier (wife): background of, 54; children of, 56, 76, 84; letters to Winston from, 69; political beliefs of, 56; relationship with Winston of, 66
Churchill, Lord Randolph (father), 7, 9, 15, 19, 22
Churchill, Winston Spencer: in America, 46, 84-85, 104-105, 112-113, 117; appearance of, 5; birth of, 7; cabinet positions held by, 58, 60-61, 62-66, 71, 80-81, 94-95; in the British Army, 23, 28-29; childhood of, 9-10, 21; as a Conservative member of Parliament, 44, 49-50, 51-52, 73, 80, 84, 89, 117; and Ireland, 74; in Cuba, 27; daily schedule of, 86; death of, 118; education of, 10-13, 15, 29; funeral of, 119; at Harrow, 14-16, 18-19; as an honorary American citizen, 117; as Knight of the Garter, 116; as a Liberal member of Parliament, 53-54, 57; marriage of, 56; medals presented to, 71; and the Middle East, 75-76; and the Nobel prize, 114; and painting, 66, 68-69, 76, 86-87, 114; political campaigns of, 34, 44, 79-80; as prime minister (1940-1945), 6, 95-98, 100, 104, 106, 108, 111; as prime minister (1951-1955), 114-116, 118; as a prisoner of war, 38-39; relationship with his children of, 67, 77; at Sandhurst, 19, 21, 22; in South Africa, 37-38, 39-41; speeches of, 5-6, 33, 45, 50, 82, 88, 91, 93, 96, 98, 99, 100, 103, 105, 107, 113
Cockran, Bourke, 46, 48, 51
Collins, Michael, 74
Conservative party, 33
Constitutionalist party, 79
Cuba, 25-26
D-Day, 107, 108
The Decline and Fall of the Roman Empire, 30
Dundee, Scotland, 54, 76

Dunkirk, France, 97
Eden, Anthony, 116
Edward VII (king of England), 49
Eisenhower, Dwight D., 106, 108, 117, 118
Elizabeth II (queen of England), 115, 117
Everest, Mrs., 9, 25
Fourth Hussars, 23, 31
Gallipoli, 66
George V (king of England), 115
George, David Lloyd, 50, 69, 71
Great Depression, the, 83, 85
Hitler, Adolf, 83, 89, 90, 91, 92, 94, 98, 103
House of Commons, 34
House of Lords, 34
India, 28, 30
iron curtain, 113
Jerome, Jenny (mother), 7, 26, 76
Kaiser Wilhelm II, 59
Kitchener, Lord Earl, 32, 65
Lays of Ancient Rome, 18
"Lawrence of Arabia," 75
London Daily Graphic, 26
London Daily Mail, 33, 36
London to Ladysmith, 42
Lord Salisbury, 31
MacDonald, Ramsay, 82, 83, 89
MacMillan, Harold, 118
"Man of the Century," 114

Marshall, George, 106
My Early Years, 85
North Atlantic Treaty Organization (NATO), 116
Oldham, England, 34, 44
parliamentary system, 34
Pearl Harbor, Hawaii, 104
Pershing, John, 71
Rhodes, Sir Cecil, 36
River War, The, 32
Rommel, Erwin, 105
Roosevelt, Franklin, 98, 102, 103, 104, 107
Saint Paul's Cathedral, 119
South Africa, 35
Stalin, Joseph, 110
Story of the Malakand Field Force, The, 31
suffragettes, 53
Twain, Mark, 46
V for Victory, 100-101
Victoria (queen of England), 49
Westminster Abbey, 56
Westminster College, 112
Whirling Dervishes, 32
"wilderness years," 83, 87
World Crisis, The, 78
World War I, 56, 58, 59, 62, 67, 72
World War II, 6, 104-105, 106, 108, 113
Yalta conference, 108